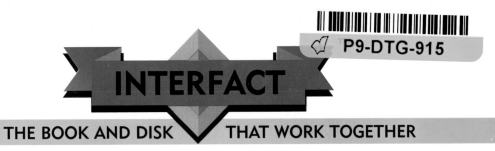

INTERFACT

THE BOOK AND DISK ⟋ THAT WORK TOGETHER

RAIN FORESTS

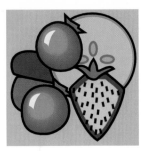

World Book

in association with

WCN

Published in the United States and Canada by
World Book, Inc.
525 W. Monroe Street, Chicago, IL 60661, USA

ISBN: 0-7166-7232-4 (Mac)
ISBN: 0-7166-7231-6 (PC)
ISBN: 0-7166-7230-8 (CD)

For information on other World Book products, call 1-800-255-1750, x 2238,
or visit us at our Web site at http://www.worldbook.com.

Created by
Two-Can Publishing Ltd,
346 Old Street, London, EC1V 9NQ

Disk
Creative Director: Jason Page
Programming Director: Brett Cropley
Art Director: Sarah Evans
Senior Designer: James Evans
Consultant: Terry Hudson
Illustrators: Rhiannon Cackett, Jeffrey Lewis,
Carlo Tartaglia, Nick Ward, Simon Woolford
Sub Editor: Jo Keane
Production Manager: Joya Bart-Plange
Special thanks to: Karen Ingebretsen and Patricia Ohlenroth, World Book Publishing

Book
Creative Director: Jason Page
Editor: Kate Graham
Assistant Editor: Jo Keane
Art Director: Belinda Webster
Designers: Michele Egar, David Oh
Author: Lucy Baker
Consultant: Roger Hammond,
Director of Living Earth
Illustrations: Francis Mosley
Story Illustrations: Valerie McBride
Production Manager: Joya Bart-Plange
Special thanks to: Karen Ingebretsen and Patricia Ohlenroth, World Book Publishing

Photograph Credits: Front cover Planet Earth Pictures
p. 9 Bruce Coleman, p. 11 (top) Heather Angel/Biofotos (bottom) South American Pictures/Tony Morrison, p. 12 Bruce Coleman/E. & P. Bauer, p. 13 Ardea/Pat Morris, p. 14 (top) Ardea/Anthony & Elizabeth Bomford (bottom) Bruce Coleman/J. Mackinnon, p.15 (top) NHPA/L.H. Newman (center) Survival Anglia/Claude Steelman (right) NHPA/Jany Sauvanet Library/J. Von Puttkamer, p. 16 (bottom) Ardea (top) Bruce Coleman, p. 17 Bruce Coleman, p. 18 The Hutchinson Library/J. Von Puttkamer, p. 19 (top) Survival International Steve Cox (bottom) The Hutchinson Library/J. Von Puttkamer, p. 20 Bruce Coleman/Michael Fogden, p. 21 Survival International Victor Englebert, p. 22 Impact Photos, p. 23 The Hutchinson Library p. 24-25 NHPA, p. 26 Oxford Scientific Films/R.A. Acharya, p. 27 South American Pictures/Bill Leimbach, p. 35 Impact/Julie Eckhardt

3 4 5 6 7 8 9 10 01 00 99

INTERFACT ™

THE BOOK AND DISK THAT WORK TOGETHER

INTERFACT will have you hooked in minutes – and that's a fact!

⬤ **The disk is packed with interactive activities, puzzles, quizzes, and games that are fun to do and packed with interesting facts.**

Try building an interactive food web and discover what different creatures eat.

Dead plants and animals

⬤ **Open the book and discover more fascinating information highlighted with lots of full-color illustrations and photographs.**

Gifts from the forest

Rain forest tribes can get everything they need from their homeland. The many different plants and animals found in the forest provide raw materials for meals, houses, clothes, medicines, tools and cosmetics.

We also use rainforest products. Many of the fruits, nuts and cereals that fill our supermarket shelves originated in the rain forest. The domestic chicken, which is now farmed worldwide, began life on the forest floor. The most expensive **hardwoods**, such as teak, mahogany and ebony, come from rainforest trees.

Other rain forest products include tea, coffee, cocoa, rubber and many types of medicine.

We still know very little about the rain forests. Scientists believe there are thousands of future foodstuffs, medicines and other raw materials waiting to be discovered.

▼ These frogs produce a strong poison under their skin to stop other animals from eating them. Some tribes extract this poison by roasting the frogs and collecting their sweat. They use it to tip their blow-pipe darts when they hunt.

● A quarter of all medicines owe their origins to rainforest plants and animals.

● Rainforest insects could offer an alternative to expensive pesticides. In Florida, three kinds of wasp were successfully introduced to control pests that were damaging the citrus trees.

● There are at least 1,500 potential new fruits and vegetables growing in the world's rainforests.

▲ Yanomami tribesmen hunt game, while women search the forest floor for food.

Read up and find out about all the products of the rain forest.

⬤ To get the most out of **INTERFACT,** use the book and disk together. Look out for the special signs called Disk Links and Bookmarks. To find out more, turn to page 43.

23

BOOKMARK

DISK LINK
How can we use rain forest plants? Find out when you play Flora Flip.

Once you've launched **INTERFACT,** you'll never look back.

LOAD UP!
Go to **page 40** to find out how to load your disks and click into action.

HELP SCREEN

Learn how to use the disk in no time at all.

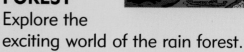

Welcome to the

INTERFACT

disk on Rain Forests

To look at all the different things on the disk, simply click the arrow keys with your mouse.

As you do this, you'll see a description of each activity in the text box.

Click on the picture at the top of the screen to select the activity you want to investigate.

These are the controls the Help Screen will tell you how to use:

- arrow keys
- reading boxes
- "hot" words

A rain forest creature that feeds on what other animals leave behind is called a...

SCAVE--E-

ROAM AROUND THE RAIN FOREST

Explore the exciting world of the rain forest.

Throw yourself into the deepest, darkest depths of the rain forest with this interactive screen. Be careful where you click your mouse – who knows what might be lurking there!

FOOD FOR THOUGHT

What is a food web and how does it keep the rain forest alive?

Learn about the eating habits of rain forest animals by building a forest food web. Discover which creatures are prey and which are predators.

WHAT'S THE WORD

Save the monkey by guessing the mystery rain forest word.

Think fast to save the monkey from the jaws of the hungry snake! Figure out the mystery rain forest words before the monkey becomes a tasty snack!

CREATE A RAIN FOREST

Design and build the rain forest of your dreams!

Design your own lush rain forest, full of plants and creatures! Select which items you want to use, position them, then print out your picture, color it, and keep it.

IT'S A JUNGLE OUT THERE

What does the future hold for the world's rain forests?

Meet Terrence the tamarin and Rosa the scarlet macaw! Terrence has the answers to all Rosa's questions about rain forests. Just click your mouse to find out more.

FLORA FLIP

Name the plants and learn about their uses.

Play this interactive card game and match the plants with their names. Once you've got them all right, you'll discover how useful they really are.

GO BANANAS!

Are you an all-around rain forest expert?

Put your knowledge of the rain forest to the test and see how many bananas you can earn. Then enter a banana-throwing competition!

What's in the book

Looking at rain forests

Imagine a forest unchanged for 60 million years, where giant trees reach up to the sky, their leafy branches blocking light from the forest floor below. Imagine a place where the temperature hardly changes from day to night, season to season, and year to year. A place where rain clouds hang in the air and heavy downpours are common. The rain forest is that amazing place.

Inside the rain forest, more than half of all species of land-based animals and plants can be found. People have lived deep in the heart of rain forests for thousands of years, too.

DISK LINK
Have a wild time planting your own lush tropical rain forest in Create a Rain Forest.

DID YOU KNOW?

● Rain forests are the wettest lands in the world. As much as 260 inches (660 cm) of rain may fall during a single year in some places.

● Almost half of all rain forests have been cut down since the 1940's, and the destruction goes on. As many as 50 million acres (20 million hectares) are destroyed every year.

LAYERS OF THE RAIN FOREST

Most rain forest life is found about 130 feet (40 m) above the ground, in a layer called the **canopy**. This is where the branches of the giant trees tangle to form a lush, green platform.

Underneath the canopy, little grows in the dim light. Where light does break through, smaller plants compete for space. Leaves that flutter down from the canopy are converted into food by insects and animals.

canopy

understory

forest floor

Where in the world

More than half of the world's rain forests are located in South America and Central America. The rest are in parts of Africa, Asia, and Australia. Almost all rain forests lie in the tropics, a region between the imaginary line north of the **equator** called the **Tropic of Cancer,** and the imaginary line south of the equator called the **Tropic of Capricorn**.

It has been hot and wet in the tropics for millions of years. These constant conditions have made it possible for rain forests to develop into the most diverse and complex **environments** in the world. Some scientists recognize more than 40 different types of rain forest, each with its own variety of plant and animal life.

Rain forests once formed a wide, green belt around the planet. But today, pictures taken from space tell a different story. All around the world, large areas of rain forest are vanishing as people clear away trees to make room for crops, homes, and businesses. As the trees are being cut down, many species of wildlife are disappearing, too.

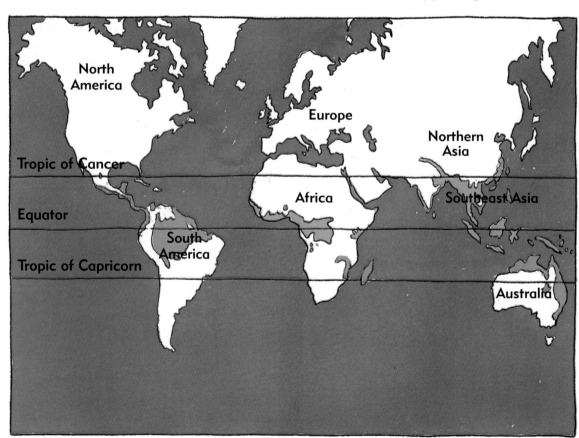

North America

Europe

Northern Asia

Tropic of Cancer

Africa

Southeast Asia

Equator

South America

Tropic of Capricorn

Australia

▶ In the tropics, the only change in the weather is from wet to wetter. This means that rain forest trees do not need to flower in spring or shed their leaves in autumn. Each type of tree has a different growth cycle, which guarantees a regular supply of fruits, nuts, and seeds for all the forest creatures.

▼ The world's largest rain forest stretches across the Amazon Basin in South America. It covers an area nearly as big as Australia. The Amazon River, which snakes through this rain forest, forms the main waterway in the largest river system in the world.

The plant bank

In the rain forest, more than 280 species of trees may grow in 2½ acres (1 ha) of land. Rain forests contain a huge variety of other plants, too. Exotic herbs and ferns flourish where light reaches the forest floor.

The canopy is like a huge garden in the sky. Climbers and vines with wiry stems hang around the giant tree trunks. Their leaves and flowers add to the lush growth in the canopy. Mosses, lichens, and orchids cover the branches. Many of these are **epiphytes,** or plants that live on other plants. Their roots dangle freely or grow in a thin layer of nutritious matter that collects in the cracks of branches.

▲ The rafflesia grows on the forest floor in parts of Asia. It produces flowers up to 3 feet (1 m) across – the biggest in the world. They have thick, warty petals and spiky centers that stink of rotting meat.

▶ Water collects in some epiphytes and provides ponds for tiny rain forest frogs.

DISK LINK
Find out more about the rain forest's exotic plants and put your memory to the test by playing Flora Flip.

PLANT FACTS

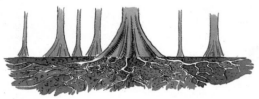

● Rain forest trees have shallow root systems, so they often produce special **buttress roots** to help keep themselves standing upright.

● Most rain forest leaves are thick and waxy, with special **drip tips** to drain away water. They are often so big they can be used as umbrellas.

Feasting in the forest

The lush vegetation of the rain forest is home to millions of different insects and other animals. Some, such as flies and beetles, act as cleaners, clearing the forest floor of debris. Others, such as wasps and bees, help to pollinate the flowers of the forest. There are lots of ants and spiders, too. They eat many other insects and so keep them from becoming too plentiful.

The plants and insects of the rain forest provide thousands of different animals with food to eat. Here are some of them.

▲ Lizards live all over the rain forest, eating insects, plants, and occasionally small animals. Most lizards seize insects in their mouths, but a few snatch them from the air with their extra-long tongues.

◄ Orangutans, found in the rain forests of Borneo and Sumatra in Southeast Asia, have huge appetites. They love fruit, but also chew leaves, shoots, and tree bark and sometimes take eggs from birds' nests. Orangutans' long, powerful arms and hook-shaped hands make swinging through the treetops easy work.

DISK LINK
Read these pages carefully. Then show off your brain power in Go Bananas!

▲ Bats are common in the rain forests. They are the world's only flying mammals. Many bats hunt insects, but some, such as the flying fox above, eat fruit. Fruit bats help to spread seeds around the forest.

▲ The hummingbird's long, thin bill is ideal for reaching the sweet nectar found inside flowers, but these birds also eat insects. Hummingbirds are flying experts and even can fly backward!

▶ Sloths have a strict leaf-eating diet. They spend practically all their time in the treetops. There are two-toed sloths and three-toed sloths, such as the one here. Algae and insects live in the sloth's fur.

Forest fiends

The rain forest is a dangerous place. The chattering monkeys, slumbering sloths, and brightly colored parrots may seem carefree, but they have their enemies. When a giant eagle soars overhead or a stealthy snake is on the prowl, the whole canopy is gripped with terror.

Eagles, along with big cats such as jaguars and leopards, are the largest hunters in the rain forest, but there are hundreds of others. In the canopy, long, slender tree snakes catch lizards, frogs, and small birds. On the forest floor, huge, heavy constrictors, such as the anaconda, wait for larger prey, such as wild boar or deer that forage in the leaf litter.

Some of the most deadly creatures are the smaller ones. Scorpions, spiders, bees, and wasps are found all over the forest. Many have poisonous bites or stings that can cause rashes, sickness, or, in extreme circumstances, death.

▲ Each rain forest has its own type of eagle. In Africa it is the crowned eagle, in South America it is the harpy eagle, and in Asia, it is the monkey-eating eagle, shown here. Eagles catch monkeys and sloths in the canopy layer.

◀ Some forest cats, such as margays, chase squirrels through the **understory**. Others, such as this jaguar, wait on low branches and pounce on passing animals underneath.

◀ The feared bushmaster hunts small animals that **scavenge** on the South American forest floor.

DISK LINK
Food for Thought will tell you which animal is at the top of the food web.

PROTECTION FROM PERIL

● The smallest rain forest creatures have the greatest number of natural enemies, so it is not surprising that they have developed many ways to defend themselves, including **camouflage**.

● Some creatures produce a poison that makes them unpleasant to eat. Bold markings advertise the fact, and predators learn to recognize the warning signs.

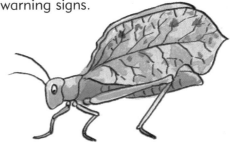

● Some moths have hidden eyespots on their wings. They flash these false eyes, startling their attackers, so that the moth may be able to escape.

● Bush crickets disguise themselves as leaves to reduce the risk of being eaten.

Rain forest people

Outsiders may be uncomfortable in the rain forest. Many find the hot, humid conditions stifling. Every step they take is fraught with danger and although there is food all around them, they probably cannot tell a poisonous berry from a nutritious and refreshing fruit.

Certain groups of people have lived in the rain forests for thousands of years. To them, the rain forest is home and the only world they know. Rain forest people live in structured communities with their own cultures and customs. They have a very deep understanding of the way the rain forests work. They know which plants and animals are useful and how to take from the forest without harming it.

There are rain forest people in parts of Africa, Asia, and South America, but their way of life is threatened. Although international laws give them rights, they are often mistreated and their land is stolen or invaded. If all these ancient peoples disappear, their knowledge of the rain forest may be lost forever.

▼ Some rain forest people build communal houses where many families live together, below. A large area of rain forest can support only a few hundred people.

◀ Rain forest children do not have to go to school, but they still have a lot to learn. Their elders must teach them everything there is to know about life in the rain forest.

▼ Many rain forest people paint their bodies with colorful dyes and use feathers, flowers, and other natural materials to make simple pieces of jewelry.

PEOPLE FACTS

● The Pygmy people of the African rain forest are very small. The tallest of them are only about 4 feet 8 inches (1.4 m) tall.

● Life is not easy in the rain forest. A person in the modern world may live for more than 70 years. In the rain forest, few people survive more than 40 years. Diseases introduced by European settlers, such as flu and measles, are still big killers of rain forest people. More than 80 different groups have died out in Brazil since 1900.

DISK LINK
Word Up! quizzes you on the new words in this book – at least one of them is on this page!

Gifts from the forest

Rain forest people can get everything they need from their homeland. The many different plants and animals found in the forest provide raw materials for meals, houses, clothes, medicines, tools, and cosmetics.

The rest of the world also uses rain forest products. Many of the fruits, nuts, and cereals that fill supermarket shelves originated in the rain forest. The ancestors of chickens, which are now farmed all over the world, began life on the rain forest floor. The most lovely, expensive **hardwoods**, such as teak, mahogany, and ebony, come from rain forest trees. Other rain forest products include tea, coffee, cocoa, rubber, bananas, and many types of medicine.

We still know very little about the rain forests. Scientists believe there are thousands of future foodstuffs, medicines, and other raw materials waiting to be discovered.

▼ These frogs produce a strong poison to stop other animals from eating them. Some rain forest people extract this poison by roasting the frogs and collecting their sweat. They use it to tip their blow-pipe darts when they hunt.

RAIN FOREST TREASURES

● There is an Amazonian tree that produces a sap very similar to diesel fuel. It can be poured straight into a truck's tank and used as fuel.

● A quarter of all medicines owe their origins to rain forest plants and animals.

● Rain forest insects could offer an alternative to expensive pesticides. In Florida, three kinds of wasps were successfully introduced to control pests that were damaging the citrus trees.

● At least 1,500 fruits and vegetables that could become popular new foods now grow in the world's rain forests.

▲ Yanomami men hunt game, while women search the forest floor for food.

Rain forest destruction

Rain forests are natural treasure houses, but they are being destroyed for timber and the land on which they stand. This happens because most rain forests grow in poor, developing countries. These countries cannot afford to keep their beautiful forests.

Large areas of rain forest are sold to timber companies. They send bulldozers and chainsaw gangs into the forest to cut down the hardwood trees. The wildlife flees and although only the oldest and largest trees are felled, more than half of the forest may be damaged by the time all the work is finished.

Rain forests are cleared completely to reach rich mineral reserves, such as iron, copper, or uranium, or to make huge cash-crop plantations of coffee, cocoa, or bananas.

Big business is only half the story. Thousands of poor, homeless people in rain forest countries are encouraged to leave the overcrowded cities and farm pieces of rain forest land. They are called **slash-and-burn** farmers because they build simple homesteads in the forest and then burn the surrounding vegetation to enrich the soil.

DISK LINK
Learn more about rain forest destruction when you play It's a Jungle Out There.

▼ About 500 million people have moved into the rain forests. These newcomers clear the forest to farm small areas of land.

DID YOU KNOW?

● Industrial countries buy more than 18 times more hardwood today than they did 50 years ago.

● More than half of Central America's rain forests are gone. They have been cleared to build huge cattle ranches. Much of the meat produced is sold to Western countries to feed the demands of their growing beef markets.

▶ See the difference between the distant lush, green rain forest and the lifeless, cracked earth in the foreground. Huge areas of Brazil have been devastated, and animals and plants are gone forever.

23

Paradise lost

It can take less than 10 years for rain forest land to become as barren and lifeless as a desert. This is because most rain forests grow in poor clay soils. Only a thin layer of rich **topsoil** covers the forest floor.

The topsoil is anchored down by the giant trees. When slash-and-burn farmers clear rain forest land to grow their crops, they destroy the trees that are needed to keep the soil in place. After only a few years, the tropical rains wash the topsoil away and the land becomes unable to support crops.

FROM SMOKE TO CHOKE

● Trees and plants help clean the air. To make food, they use sunlight, water, and the carbon dioxide that we breathe out. In this process, they produce the oxygen that we breathe in.

When rain forests are burned to clear land, the fires create carbon dioxide that pollutes the air. Also, the fewer trees there are, the less oxygen there is for people to live on.

The wastelands left by slash-and-burn farmers are baked dry by the sun and then drenched by the heavy rains. The rains, which would have watered the thirsty trees and plants, now fall straight to the ground and run downhill, carrying tons of soil with them. Valleys are flooded and rivers become clogged with mud.

Scientists believe that, at the present rate of destruction, there will be no rain forests left by the year 2030. If this paradise is lost, thousands of different plants, trees, and animals will disappear forever.

Save the rain forests

More and more people are becoming aware of the need to save the rain forests. Some steps already have been taken to slow the rate of destruction. Rain forest people have blocked the path of bulldozers and chainsaw gangs, and many **conservation** groups have launched huge campaigns.

Much more still could be done. Timber companies could change the way they harvest the forest, to reduce the damage they cause. They also could replant areas of forest that have been disturbed. Slash-and-burn farmers could be taught to plant trees along with their crops to preserve the fragile topsoil and use the same land for many years.

Rich industrial countries could help, too. They could reduce the debts owed to them by rain forest countries, which use their forestland to clear the debts. That way, at least the remaining forests could be preserved.

DISK LINK
Bet you can't guess what the orangutan's name means. Roam Around the Rain Forest and make it one of your discoveries!

▲ The Kayapo Indians live in the Amazon rain forest in Brazil. Their traditional dress includes a piece of wood called a lip-plate, which members of the tribe wear in holes cut into their lower lips. The Kayapo have campaigned to save the forest and their way of life from gold miners.

◀ Scientists believe that more than 50 wild species of plants and animals become extinct every day because of rain forest destruction. Many of our favorite animals, such as tigers and orangutans, are at risk because their homes are being destroyed. By protecting rain forests, they could be saved from **extinction**.

RAIN FOREST ACTION

● Spread the word

Tell your friends and relatives about the plight of the rain forests. Write to the government and ask it to help rain forest countries.

● Support rain forest campaigns

Many charities and action groups work to convince countries to slow down the rate of rain forest destruction. They need money and support. Watch for news on television and radio and in newspapers and magazines about how you can help them.

The cowrie thieves

For thousands of years, people have told stories
about the world around them. Often these stories try
to explain something that people do not understand, such as how
the world began, or where light comes from. This tale is
told by the people of the Congo in Africa.

Long ago, in a village right in the middle
of the Congo, there lived a man and his
wife who were always causing mischief.

All the other villagers agreed that this
mischievous man and his mischievous
wife had the most irritating habits. They
hardly ever did any work, preferring to sit
around and chatter to each other. When
they did start to work, they would tire of
whatever they were doing very quickly and
wander off to find something else to do.

They were always dropping in at their
neighbors' huts just when dinner was
ready. Their neighbors were obliged to
ask them in to supper, since that was
the local custom. But the worst thing
of all was the way they would pick up
other people's belongings.

The two of them would just wander
into other people's huts and start picking
up anything that they could see. They
would poke their noses into baskets, help
themselves to a mouthful of food, or just
move everything around so that the
owner of the hut would come home to a
terrible mess.

The other villagers put up with the pair because they really never did much harm. Whenever a villager lost his temper with them, they looked so hurt at the thought that they had done wrong and promised so fervently to mend their ways that it was impossible to be angry for long.

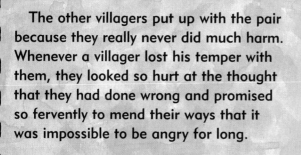

One day, however, the mischievous man and his mischievous wife wandered into the hut of an important man in the village and pulled his bag of cowrie shells out from under his bed. Cowrie shells were very valuable to the Congo people, and this bag held all the man's wealth. The mischievous couple spilled the cowrie shells onto the floor and began to play with them, rolling them around and tossing them to each other.

Eventually the mischievous man decided to go find some food, and his mischievous wife followed him, leaving the cowrie shells just as they were, all over the floor.

When the owner of the hut came back and saw his cowrie shells scattered about, he thought he had been robbed.

The important man shouted to all the other villagers to come and see what had happened. The woman from the hut next door told him that she had seen the mischievous man and his mischievous wife coming out of his hut.

Just then, another villager spotted the mischievous couple coming around the corner with a bunch of bananas. They looked very surprised when they were accused of stealing the cowrie shells.

The important man who thought he had been robbed did not wait for an explanation. "Just you wait until I get you!" he yelled.

He rushed at the pair, waving his arms fiercely. The mischievous man and his mischievous wife ran as fast as they could into the shelter of the forest, with all the villagers chasing after them.

When they reached the forest, the mischievous man and his mischievous wife climbed up a tree to hide from the villagers. For a few minutes the villagers were puzzled. Then one of them spotted the mischievous wife's hair hanging down from a branch.

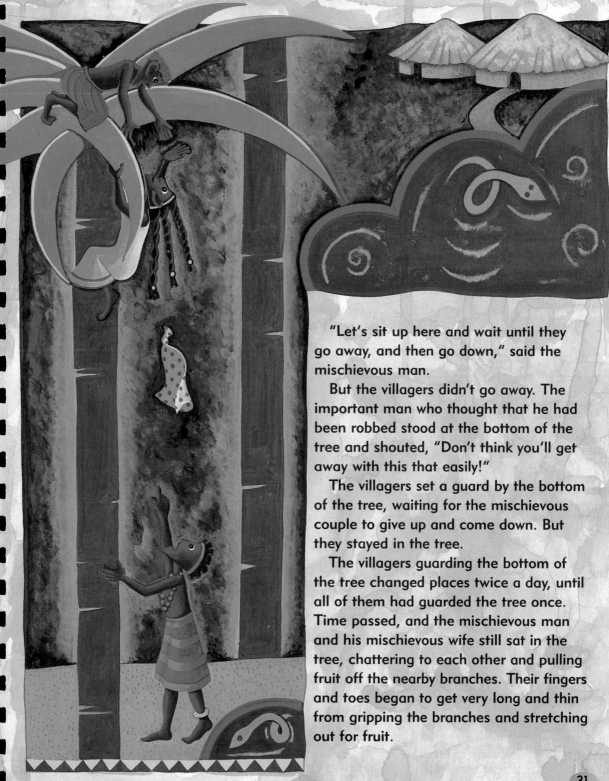

"Let's sit up here and wait until they go away, and then go down," said the mischievous man.

But the villagers didn't go away. The important man who thought that he had been robbed stood at the bottom of the tree and shouted, "Don't think you'll get away with this that easily!"

The villagers set a guard by the bottom of the tree, waiting for the mischievous couple to give up and come down. But they stayed in the tree.

The villagers guarding the bottom of the tree changed places twice a day, until all of them had guarded the tree once. Time passed, and the mischievous man and his mischievous wife still sat in the tree, chattering to each other and pulling fruit off the nearby branches. Their fingers and toes began to get very long and thin from gripping the branches and stretching out for fruit.

One day, when all the villagers had guarded the bottom of the tree twice, the mischievous man and his mischievous wife realized that the hair on their bodies had grown long and thick, making it hard for them to be seen in the branches.

Much later, when all the villagers had guarded the bottom of the tree three times, the mischievous man and his mischievous wife felt a tingle at the bottom of their spines. They had grown tails! They swung about with their new tails and jumped up and down on their branch, chattering to each other so fast that what they said no longer sounded like human speech.

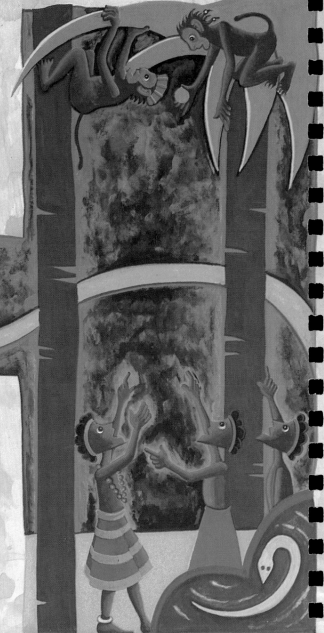

The villager guarding the tree heard all the noise and stared up at the pair. What a surprise he got! The mischievous man and his mischievous wife had turned into monkeys!

When the villager went back to the village to tell the others what he had seen, the important man who thought he had been robbed was furious. But later, when he had counted his cowrie shells, he realized how unjust he had been. How he regretted his hastiness!

And that is why, even though the people of the Congo are often annoyed with the mischievous monkeys that come into their houses and make a mess or take their food, they never do them harm.

True or false?

Which of these facts are true and which are false?
If you have read this book carefully, you will know the answers!

1. Rain forests grow all over Europe.

2. Rain forests lie between the tropics of Capricorn and Cancer.

3. Some scientists recognize up to 40 kinds of rain forests.

4. Algae live in the fur of sloths.

5. More than 280 tree species may grow in 2½ acres (1 ha) of rain forest.

6. The world's largest rain forest is in Australia.

7. Orangutans live in the forests of Africa.

8. Eagles feed mainly on animals that live on the forest floor.

9. Chickens originally came from the rain forest.

10. Rain forest people collect poison from frogs by squeezing them.

11. Sap from an Amazonian tree can be used as diesel fuel in trucks.

12. All the world's rain forests may be destroyed by the year 2030.

13. Slash-and-burn farming helps the rain forest grow.

ANSWERS: 1.F 2.T 3.T 4.T 5.T 6.F 7.F 8.F 9.T 10.F 11.T 12.T 13.F

Glossary

● **Buttress roots** develop on tall rain forest trees to support their heavy trunks and help them stay upright.

● **Camouflage** is what makes certain rain forest creatures hard to see. Their bodies have patterns, shapes, or colors – or all three – that match their surroundings. These help hide them from predators. A chameleon even can change its body color to blend in with its surroundings.

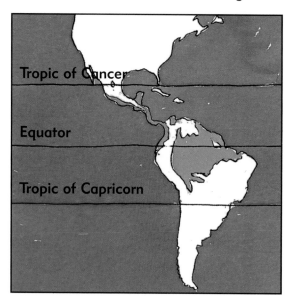

Tropic of Cancer

Equator

Tropic of Capricorn

● **Canopy** is the uppermost layer of the rain forest, the dense, leafy section some 20 to 23 feet (6 to 7 m) deep, at 130 to 165 feet (40 to 50 m) above the ground. Most rain forest animals live in this layer.

● **Conservation** is the preservation of natural species and environments from exploitation by humans.

● **Drip tip** is the long tip on most leaves in the rain forest, developed to shed rain from the leaf's waxy surface.

● **Environment** is the special combination of conditions in an area. This combination determines the types of plants and animals that can live there.

● **Epiphyte** is a plant that grows on another plant without damaging it. It is not a parasite, which harms its host.

● **Equator** is the imaginary line lying exactly halfway between the North and South poles. Most of the world's tropical rain forests grow directly north or south of this line.

● **Extinction** occurs when the last member of an animal or plant species dies out because of overhunting, a change in its habitat, or failure to compete with a new arrival in its environment.

● **Hardwood** trees such as ebony, teak, and mahogany grow in the rain forest. Their tough wood is excellent for making strong furniture and is in great demand. This is one cause of the destruction of large parts of the rain forest.

● **Scavenger** is a creature that feeds on the waste left by others, for instance, on the scaps of another animal's kill.

● **Tropic of Capricorn** is the southern boundary of the earth's Tropical Zone. It lies 23½ degrees south of the equator. Most rain forests grow between the Tropic of Cancer and the Tropic of Capricorn.

● **Understory** is the name for the smaller trees and bushes that make up the middle level in a rain forest, below the tops of the taller trees.

● **Slash-and-burn** describes a method of farming in which farmers clear areas of the rain forest and burn the trees to create land on which to grow their crops.

● **Topsoil** is the fertile soil that forms the top layer of earth on the rain forest floor. The trees hold the topsoil in place, but when they are cut down, the rains rapidly wash the topsoil away.

● **Tropic of Cancer** is the northern boundary of the earth's Tropical Zone. It lies 23½ degrees north of the equator. Most rain forests grow between the Tropic of Cancer and the Tropic of Capricorn.

Lab pages

Loading your INTERFACT disk

INTERFACT is available on floppy disk and CD-ROM for both PCs with Windows and Apple Macintoshes. Make sure you follow the correct instructions for the disk you have chosen and your type of computer. Before you begin, check the system requirements (inside front cover).

CD-ROM INSTRUCTIONS

If you have a copy of INTERFACT on CD, you can run the program from the disk – you don't need to install it on your hard drive.

PC WITH WINDOWS 95

1 Put the disk in the CD drive
2 Open MY COMPUTER
3 Double click on the CD drive icon
4 Double click on the icon called RAINFOR

PC WITH WINDOWS 3.1 OR 3.11

1 Put the disk in the CD drive
2 Select RUN from the FILE menu in the PROGRAM MANAGER
3 Type **D:\RAINFOR** (where D is the letter of your CD drive.
4 Press the RETURN key

MACINTOSH

1 Put the disk in the CD drive
2 Double click on the INTERFACT icon
3 Double click on the icon called RAINFOR

FLOPPY DISK INSTRUCTIONS

If you have a copy of INTERFACT on floppy disk, you must install the program on your computer's hard drive before you can run it.

PC WITH WINDOWS 95

To install INTERFACT:
1. Put the disk in the floppy drive
2. Select RUN from the START menu
3. Type **A:\INSTALL** (Where A is the letter of your floppy drive)
4. Click OK – unless you want to change the name of the Interfact directory

To run INTERFACT:
Once the program has been installed, open the START menu and select PROGRAMS, then select INTERFACT and click on the icon called RAIN FORESTS

PC WITH WINDOWS 3.1 OR 3.11

To install INTERFACT:
1. Put the disk in the floppy drive
2. Select RUN from the FILE menu in the PROGRAM MANAGER
3. Type **A:\INSTALL** (Where A is the letter of your floppy drive)
4. Click OK – unless you want to change the name of the Interfact directory

To run INTERFACT:
Once the program has been installed, open the INTERFACT group in the PROGRAM MANAGER and double click the icon called RAIN FORESTS

MACINTOSH

To install INTERFACT:
1. Put the disk in the floppy drive
2. Double click on the icon called INTERFACT INSTALLER
3. Click CONTINUE
4. Click INSTALL– unless you want to change the name of the Interfact folder

To run INTERFACT:
Once the program has been installed, open the INTERFACT folder and double click the icon called RAIN FORESTS

How to use INTERFACT

INTERFACT is easy to use.
First find out how to run the program
(see page 40), then read these simple
instructions and dive in!

You will find that there are lots of different features to explore.
Choose the feature you want to play using the controls on the right-hand side of the screen. You will see that the main area of the screen changes as you click on different features.

For example, this is what your screen will look like when you play Go Bananas, a fun-filled test of your rain forest knowledge. Once you've selected a feature, click on the main screen to start playing.

Click here to select the feature you want to play.

Click to continue

Click on the arrow keys to scroll through the different features on the disk or find your way to the exit.

This is the text box, where instructions and directions appear. See page 4 to find out what's on the disk.

DISK LINKS

When you read the book, you'll come across Disk Links. These show you where to find activities on the disk that relate to the page you are reading. Use the arrow keys to find the icon on screen that matches the one in the Disk Link.

DISK LINK
Food for Thought will tell you which animal is at the top of the food web.

BOOKMARKS

As you explore the features on the disk, you'll bump into Bookmarks. These show you where to look in the book for more information about the topic on screen. Just turn to the page of the book shown in the Bookmark.

23

LAB PAGES

On pages 36–39, you'll find grid pages to photocopy. These are for making notes and recording any thoughts or ideas you may have as you read the book.

HOT DISK TIPS

● After you have chosen the feature you want to play, remember to move the cursor from the icon to the main screen before clicking the mouse again.

● If you don't know how to use one of the on-screen controls, simply touch it with your cursor. An explanation will pop up in the text box!

● Keep a close eye on the cursor. When it changes from an arrow ➜ to a hand, click your mouse and something will happen.

● Any words that appear on screen in blue and underlined are "hot." This means you can touch them with the cursor for more information.

● Explore the screen! There are secret hot spots and hidden surprises to find.

Troubleshooting

If you have a problem with your INTERFACT disk, you should find the solution here. If you still cannot solve your problem, call the helpline at 1-800-424-1280

COMMON PROBLEMS

Cannot load disk
There is not enough space available on your hard disk. To make more space available, delete old applications and programs you don't use until 6 MB of free space is available.

There is no sound (PCs only)
Your sound card is not SoundBlaster compatible. To make your settings SoundBlaster compatible, see your sound card manual for more information.

Disk will not run
There is not enough memory available. Quit all other applications and programs. If this does not work, increase your machine's RAM by adjusting the Virtual Memory (see right).

There is no sound
Your speakers or headphones are not connected to the CD-ROM drive. Ensure that your speakers or headphones are connected to the speaker outlet at the back of your computer.

Print-outs are not centered on the page or are partly cut off
Make sure that the page layout is set to "Landscape" in the Print dialog box.

There is no sound
Ensure that the volume control is turned up (on your external speakers and by using internal volume control).

Graphics freeze or text boxes appear blank (Windows 95 or 98 only)

Graphics card acceleration is too high. Right-click on MY COMPUTER. Click on SETTINGS (Windows 95) or PROPERTIES (Windows 98), then PERFORMANCE, then GRAPHICS. Reset the hardware acceleration slider to "None." Click OK. You may have to restart your computer.

Text does not fit into boxes or hot words do not work

The standard fonts on your computer have been moved or deleted. You must reinstall them. PC users need Arial. Macintosh users need Helvetica. Please see your computer manual for further information.

Your machine freezes

There is not enough memory available. Either quit other applications and programs or increase your machine's RAM by adjusting the Virtual Memory (see right).

Graphics do not load or are of poor quality

Not enough memory is available, or you have the wrong display setting. Either quit other applications and programs or make sure that your monitor control is set to 256 colors (Mac) or VGA (PC).

HOW TO...

Reset screen resolution in Windows 3.1 or 3.11:

In Program Manager, double-click on MAIN. Double-click on OPTIONS, then click on "Change system settings." Reset the screen resolution to 640 x 480, 256 Colors. Restart your computer after changing display settings.

Reset screen resolution in Windows 95 or 98:

Click on START at the bottom left of your screen, then click on SETTINGS, then CONTROL PANEL. Then double-click on DISPLAY. Click on the SETTINGS tab at the top. Reset the Desktop area (or Display area) to 640 x 480 pixels, then click APPLY. You may need to restart your computer after changing display settings.

Reset screen resolution for Macintosh:

Click on the Apple symbol at the top left of your screen to access APPLE MENU ITEMS. Select CONTROL PANELS, then MONITORS (or MONITORS AND SOUND). Set the resolution to 640 x 480.

Adjust the Virtual Memory on a PC with Windows 95 or 98:

Open MY COMPUTER, then click on CONTROL PANEL, then SYSTEMS. Select PERFORMANCE, click on VIRTUAL MEMORY, and set the preferred size to a higher value.

Adjust the Virtual Memory on a Macintosh:

If you have 16 MB of RAM or more, GREECE will run faster. Select the GREECE icon and go to GET INFO in the FILE folder. Set the preferred (or current) size to a higher value.

Index

WORLD BOOK ENCYCLOPEDIA PRESENTS **ELECTRICITY and MAGNETISM**

EXPERIMENT with a computerized circuit

LEARN from talking electrons

INVESTIGATE aboard an interactive time machine

CD (PC/MAC) ISBN 0-7166-7209-X

WORLD BOOK ENCYCLOPEDIA PRESENTS **PLANTS**

GROW your own virtual plant on screen

DISCOVER how plants turn light into food

INVESTIGATE the different parts of a tree

CD (PC/MAC) ISBN 0-7166-7239-1

WORLD BOOK ENCYCLOPEDIA PRESENTS **SENSES**

EXPLORE the brain and the body

LEARN how each of the senses works

PLAY a sensational interactive adventure

CD (PC/MAC) ISBN 0-7166-7233-2

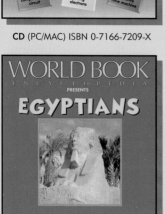

WORLD BOOK ENCYCLOPEDIA PRESENTS **EGYPTIANS**

PLAY an ancient Egyptian board game

CREATE a secret message in hieroglyphs

INVESTIGATE an interactive Egyptian wall painting

CD (PC/MAC) ISBN 0-7166-7206-5

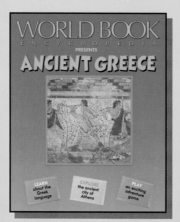

WORLD BOOK ENCYCLOPEDIA PRESENTS **ANCIENT GREECE**

LEARN about the Greek language

EXPLORE the ancient city of Athens

PLAY an exciting adventure game

CD (PC/MAC) ISBN 0-7166-7234-0

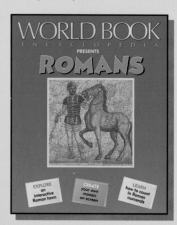

WORLD BOOK ENCYCLOPEDIA PRESENTS **ROMANS**

EXPLORE an interactive Roman town

CREATE your own mosaic on screen

LEARN how to count in Roman numerals

CD (PC/MAC) ISBN 0-7166-7215-4

WORLD BOOK ENCYCLOPEDIA PRESENTS **RAIN FORESTS**

INVESTIGATE amazing rain forest plants

EXPLORE a virtual rain forest scene

BUILD an interactive food web

CD (PC/MAC) ISBN 0-7166-7230-8

WORLD BOOK ENCYCLOPEDIA PRESENTS **POLAR LANDS**

INVESTIGATE the history of the polar regions

EXPLORE the Arctic and Antarctic landscapes

CREATE food webs for the polar animals

CD (PC/MAC) ISBN 0-7166-7227-8

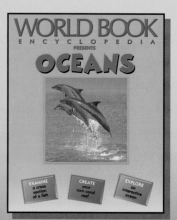

WORLD BOOK ENCYCLOPEDIA PRESENTS **OCEANS**

EXAMINE a cross section of a fish

CREATE your own coral reef

EXPLORE an interactive ocean

CD (PC/MAC) ISBN 0-7166-7212-X

WATCH FOR NEW TITLES!

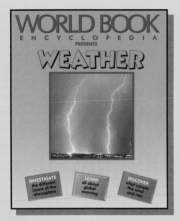

WORLD BOOK ENCYCLOPEDIA PRESENTS
WEATHER

INVESTIGATE the different layers of the atmosphere

LEARN all about global warming

DISCOVER what causes the wind and rain

CD (PC/MAC) ISBN 0-7166-7236-7

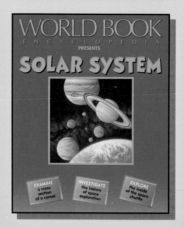

WORLD BOOK ENCYCLOPEDIA PRESENTS
SOLAR SYSTEM

EXAMINE a cross section of a comet

INVESTIGATE the history of space exploration

EXPLORE the inside of the space shuttle

CD (PC/MAC) ISBN 0-7166-7218-9

WORLD BOOK ENCYCLOPEDIA PRESENTS
SPACE TRAVEL

EXPLORE an orbiting space station

MEET famous astronauts from history

LAUNCH your own satellites into space

CD (PC/MAC) ISBN 0-7166-7202-2

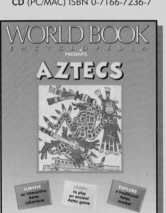

WORLD BOOK ENCYCLOPEDIA PRESENTS
AZTECS

SURVIVE an interactive Aztec adventure

LEARN to play an ancient Aztec game

EXPLORE a traditional Aztec market

CD (PC/MAC) ISBN 0-7166--7250-2

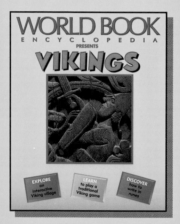

WORLD BOOK ENCYCLOPEDIA PRESENTS
VIKINGS

EXPLORE an interactive Viking village

LEARN to play a traditional Viking game

DISCOVER how to write in runes

CD (PC/MAC) ISBN 0-7166-7221-9

There is a wide array of **INTERFACT** titles to choose from, covering science, history, and nature.

And if you turn the page, you'll discover the new **INTERFACT REFERENCE** series of books and disks.

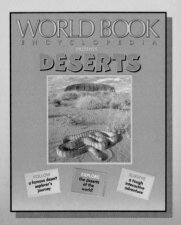

WORLD BOOK ENCYCLOPEDIA PRESENTS
DESERTS

FOLLOW a famous desert explorer's journey

EXPLORE the deserts of the world!

SURVIVE a tough interactive adventure

CD (PC/MAC) ISBN 0-7166--7203-0

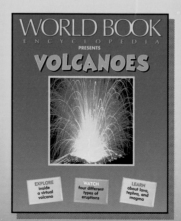

WORLD BOOK ENCYCLOPEDIA PRESENTS
VOLCANOES

EXPLORE inside a virtual volcano

WATCH four different types of eruptions

LEARN about lava, tephra, and magma

CD (PC/MAC) ISBN 0-7166-7224-3

INTERFACT REFERENCE

Look for the new **INTERFACT REFERENCE** series.
Each large, colorful book works with an exciting disk, opening up
whole new areas of learning and providing a great reference source.

CD (PC/MAC) ISBN 0-7166-9910-9   CD (PC/MAC) ISBN 0-7166-9912-5   CD (PC/MAC) ISBN 0-7166-9911-7

INTERFACT CATALOG

Welcome to the Interfact Catalog! Here, you can try out an activity from
each disk in the Interfact line. To take a look at a demo, just click on one
of these buttons. If you'd like more information about purchasing from the
Interfact series, just click on the How to Order button. And when you're
ready to leave the Interfact Catalog, just click on the Exit button.

Ancient Greece · Aztecs · Egyptians · Electricity and Magnetism · Oceans · Plants · Polar Lands
Rainforests · Romans · Senses · Solar System · Vikings · Volcanoes · Weather
Interfact Reference Atlas · HOW TO ORDER · EXIT

**Make sure that you check out
the INTERFACT Catalog on your
INTERFACT CD-ROM.**

**You'll find a feature to play
from each of the titles in
the INTERFACT series.**

For more information, **call 1-800-255-1750, x 2238,**
or visit us at our Web site at **http://www.worldbook.com.**